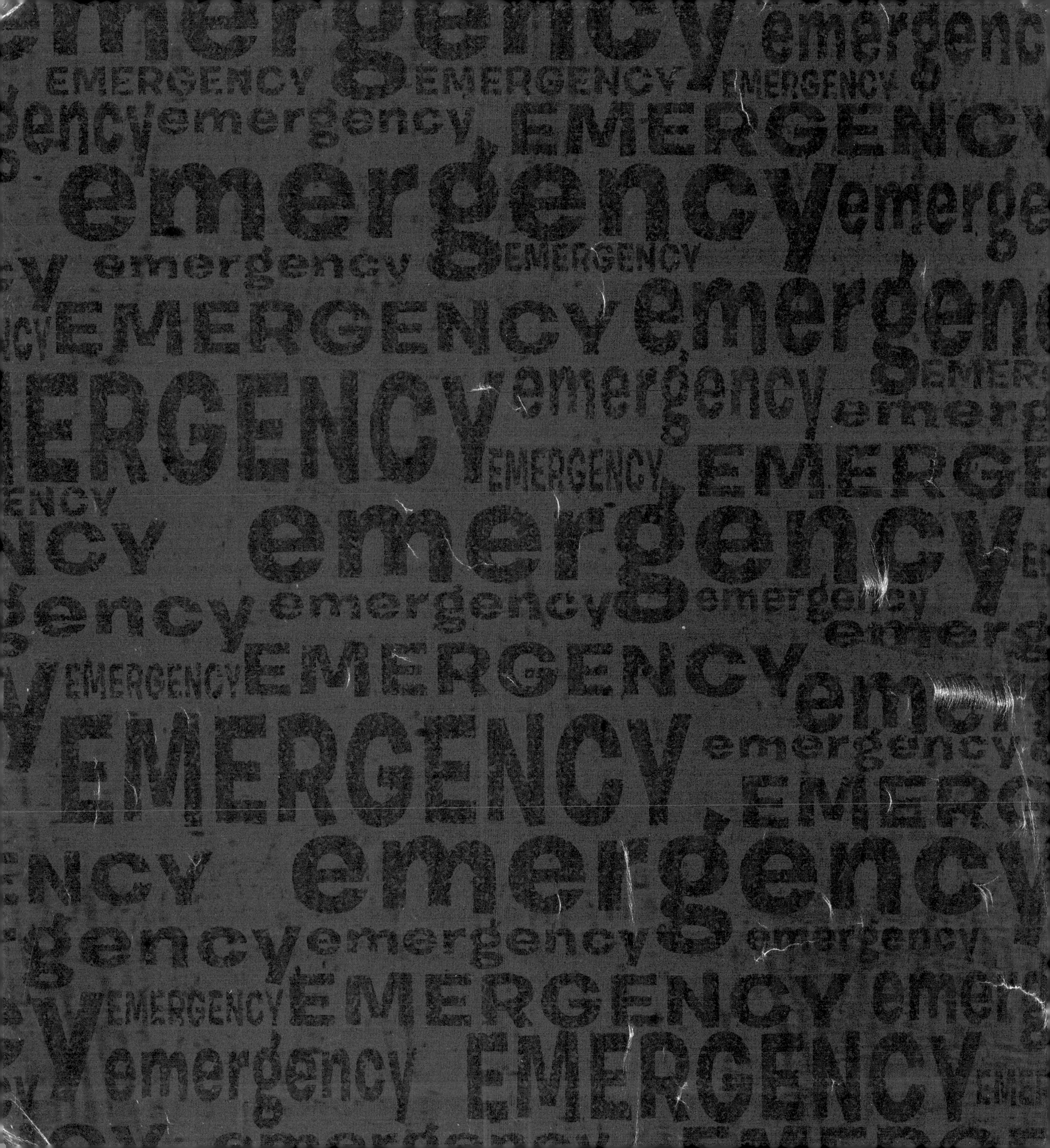

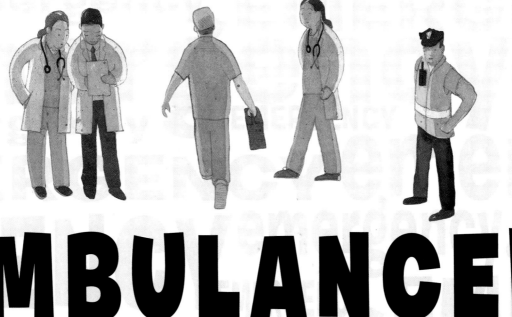

AMBULANCE! AMBULANCE!

SALLY SUTTON • ILLUSTRATED BY BRIAN LOVELOCK

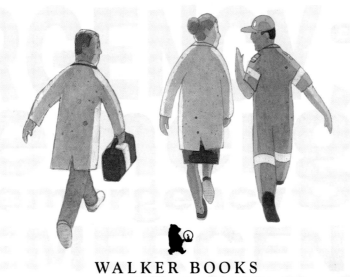

WALKER BOOKS
AND SUBSIDIARIES

LONDON • BOSTON • SYDNEY • AUCKLAND

Bleep, bleep. Emergency!
News just through:
Crash, crash, there's been a crash.
Let's go, crew!

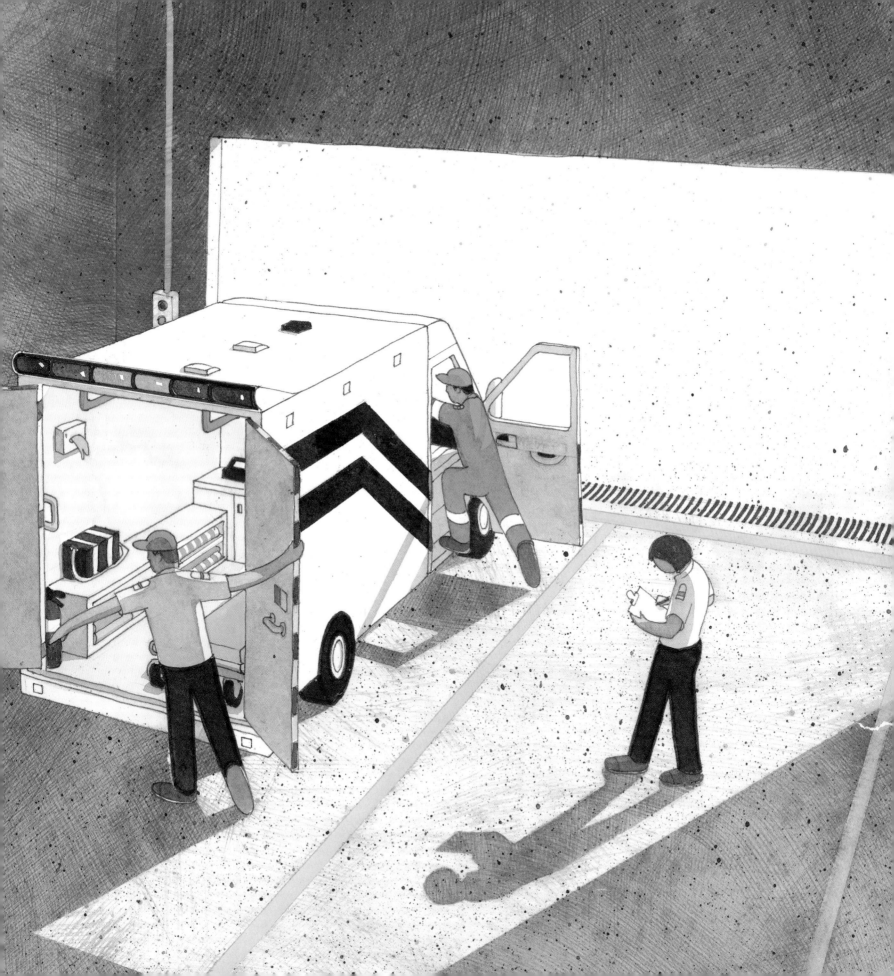

Nee nar nee nar

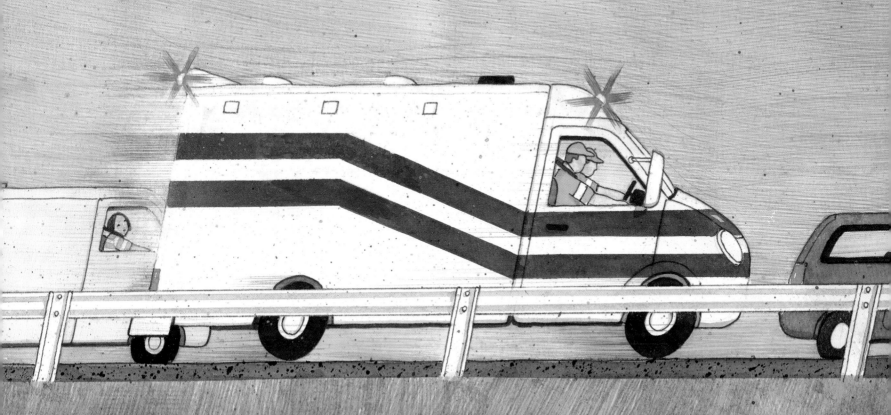

Stop, stop the ambulance.
Bump bump bump.
Grab, grab the rescue pack.
Out we jump.

Check, check the rider's heart.
Boom boom boom.
Splint, splint his broken leg.
Right! Let's zoom!

Lift, lift the stretcher in.
Slide and lock.
Call, call the hospital.
"Stand by, doc!"

Close, close the heavy doors.
Clink clank clonk.
Sound, sound the giant horn.
Honk honk honk!

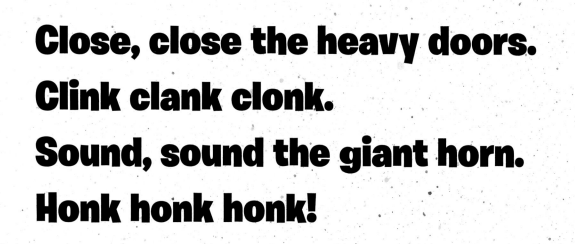

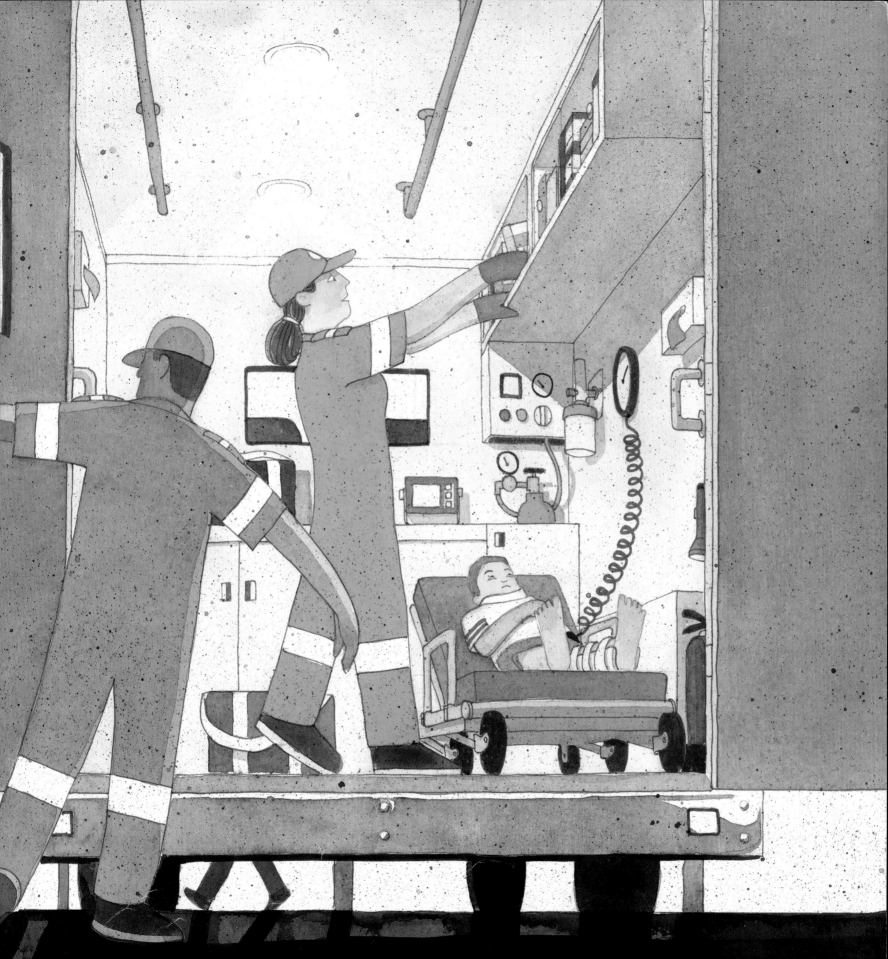

Flash, flash
the warning lights.
Flick flick flick.
Race, race to hospital.
Quick quick quick!

Nee nar nee nar

Wheel, wheel the patient in.
Teams crowd round.
Soon, soon he'll be fixed up.
Safe and sound.

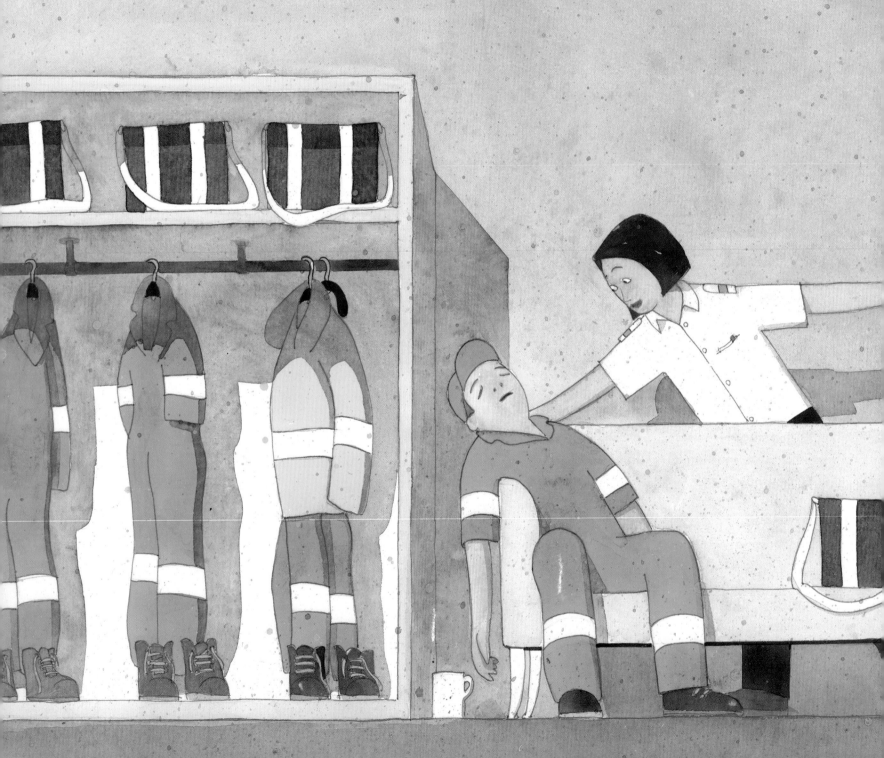

Phew, phew, let's take a break.
Then ... oh, no!
Bleep, bleep. Emergency!
Off we go...

nee nar nee nar...

For Theo, and his most
excellent Grandpa. S.S.

For Harry. B.L.

First published 2017 by Walker Books Ltd
87 Vauxhall Walk, London SE11 5HJ

10 9 8 7 6 5 4 3 2 1

Text © 2017 Sally Sutton
Illustrations © 2017 Brian Lovelock

The right of Sally Sutton and Brian Lovelock
to be identified as author and illustrator respectively
of this work has been asserted by them in accordance
with the Copyright, Designs and Patents Act 1988

This book has been typeset in Burbank Big Regular

Printed in China

British Library Cataloguing in Publication Data:
a catalogue record for this book is available from
the British Library

ISBN 978-1-4063-7428-5

www.walker.co.uk

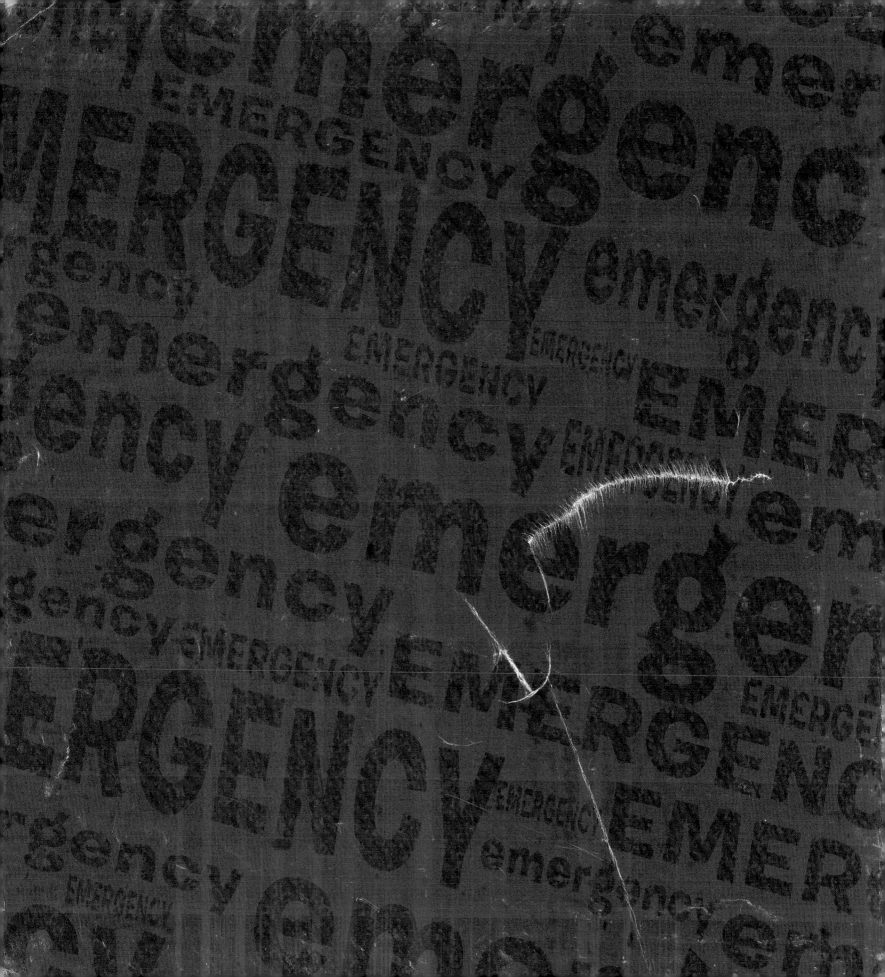